All for One!

Part 2

adapted by Michael Teitelbaum

based on the Marvel comic book series *The Mighty Avengers*

interior illustrated by Pat Olliffe and Hi-Fi Design

Reader's Digest Children's Books®

New York, New York • Montréal, Québec • Bath, United Kingdom

A short while later, Ant-Man pointed to a group of large tents below.

"There!" he announced to the others. "That's where we'll find the Hulk!"

Iron Man and the Wasp followed Ant-Man and discovered a circus. Inside one of the tents, the Hulk was juggling elephants! The crowd cheered wildly.

"This is bizarre," Iron Man said. "But he doesn't seem to be harming anyone."

The Wasp, however, saw things differently. Loki planted a vision in her mind of the Hulk getting ready to toss an enormous elephant into the crowd!

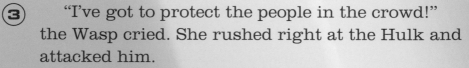

③ "I've got to protect the people in the crowd!" the Wasp cried. She rushed right at the Hulk and attacked him.

Hulk grew enraged and swatted at the Wasp.

Although they were confused about why she attacked the Hulk in the first place, Ant-Man and Iron Man sprung into action. Once the Hulk started fighting back, they knew he had to be stopped.

④

Meanwhile, as his fellow Super Heroes
battled the Hulk, Thor sped across the Rainbow
Bridge that connected Earth to Asgard.

"I must find and stop Loki," Thor said.

Thor raced to the Isle of Silence where he
knew his brother had been exiled.

5 It didn't take the Thunder God long to find Loki. "I know it is you who caused the Hulk to attack that train," Thor shouted. "What do you have to say for yourself?"

6 Loki remained silent. But a deep rumbling shook the ground beneath Thor's feet.

Suddenly, the Silent Ones, a race of underground trolls who lived on the Isle of Silence, burst from the ground. They grabbed Thor, clawing at him, trying to drag him down.

The Silent Ones were powerful beings of pure evil, but the God of Thunder was stronger. He pulled one arm free, raised his hammer, then slammed its handle into the ground.

Deep cracks spread through the ground with a mighty rumble. The Silent Ones, unused to loud noises, recoiled in pain and fled.

Having eliminated the threat of the Silent Ones, Thor once again took to the skies to track down Loki.

Thor sped all around the Isle of Silence, searching for his brother. He finally caught up to Loki at the Rainbow Bridge.

Loki planted an illusion in the mind of Hemdal, Guardian of the Rainbow Bridge. This distracted him long enough to let Loki slip past.

"You cannot outrun me, brother!" Thor shouted. "And you will answer for your mischief!"

Thor caught up to Loki and grabbed him.

"Your caring and protection for the mortals of Earth is truly pathetic, brother," Loki snarled, as Thor lifted him into the air. "You should be their ruler."

"Loki, you have never learned to respect all beings, regardless of their abilities," Thor replied. "And that is the reason for your downfall."

③   Holding Loki firmly in his grasp, Thor returned to Earth.

④   With the Wasp no longer in Loki's power, she realized that the Hulk had not placed the circus crowd in danger and managed to calm him down.

"This is Loki, my evil brother," Thor announced to the others. "This entire situation is all his fault. He planted a vision of broken train tracks into the Hulk's mind. That is why the Hulk stopped that train. He wanted to draw me out so he could escape his imprisonment, but now that plan has failed!"

But Loki's mischief was not finished yet. He put a vision in the minds of the Super Heroes, creating the illusion that there were many Lokis surrounding them.

"Which one is real?" the Hulk asked, punching wildly at one of the illusions.

Thor flung his hammer at one of the figures of Loki, but the hammer passed right through the image. Iron Man fired a repulsor blast at another Loki, but his attack also zoomed harmlessly through nothing but air.

The Wasp tried to fly right at another Loki. Instead, she ran into an invisible barrier, by Loki's mind, which stopped her in mid-flight.

6 "You foolish mortals are so easy to manipulate!" Loki cried from everywhere at once.

(7) The Hulk watched the other Super Heroes struggling as a result of Loki's trickery. Hulk suddenly realized that they were not his enemies.

The Hulk grew enraged, his anger building by the second. As all thoughts other than rage were crowded out of the Hulk's mind, so was the telepathic influence of Loki. All the false images of Loki that had been planted in the Hulk's mind disappeared. The Green

(8) Goliath was now staring at the one true Loki.

The Hulk grabbed Loki as the other heroes arrived.

"My father Odin and I will deal with my brother and his evil," Thor said.

The group started to break up.

"Wait a minute," Iron Man said. "We all have special abilities. What if we work together for the betterment of humankind?"

"I like the idea," Ant-Man said. "It felt good working with all of you to avenge a wrong."

"I know what we can call ourselves," the Wasp added. "The Avengers!"

"I would be honored to be part of this team," Thor said.

"Hulk in, too," said the Emerald Behemoth.

And so, for the first of what would be many times, the Avengers assembled.